The Cat and the Captain

The Cat and the Captain

BY ELIZABETH COATSWORTH

Illustrated by Bernice Loewenstein

MACMILLAN PUBLISHING CO., INC.
New York
COLLIER MACMILLAN PUBLISHERS
London

Library of Congress Cataloging in Publication Data
Coatsworth, Elizabeth Jane, date
[1. Cats—Fiction]   I. Loewenstein, Bernice, illus.
II. Title. PZ7.C6294Cat9   [E]   73–6041
ISBN 0–02–719070–6

This book I do especially owe
To Bobbie and I've told her so.
And all the other books I've done
Are kittens of this mother one.

Contents

1 · The Cat Was Furious   1

2 · A Good Cat at Heart   4

3 · The Face at the Window   11

4 · One Day on the "Lively Ann"   18

5 · Every Fine Morning   23

6 · "There's Trouble Coming"   29

7 · Sh! What's That?   37

8 · The Cat's First Party   41

9 · This Cat Saved Us   48

1

The Cat Was Furious

The Cat was furious. Not a door or window of the house was open. He went to the front door and mewed. He went to the side door (which was almost never used) and mewed. Then he went to the back door and there he mewed loudest and longest.

He could hear the Captain's housekeeper, Mrs. Tillie Todd, walking around the kitchen, singing to herself. She was always humming to herself like a bumblebee. When something happened to make her excited, she made up songs, mostly complaining ones telling how she felt. The Cat knew that Mrs. Tillie heard him there at her door with his feet in the damp and was glad to keep him out.

If only the Captain were home, he would call, "Mrs. Tillie! Ship ahoy! Lower the gangway to take on passengers!" But the Captain had taken his umbrella and gone to see his married daughter. Goodness only knew when he'd be back!

The Cat picked his way across the grass, shaking the wet off his feet, for it had been raining. Poor Cat, he hated it! He was thinking of the cushioned chair indoors by the fire where he loved to sit watching the flames with sleepy eyes and purring to himself. But he didn't feel like purring now. He climbed up the lilac bush. He knew just where to put each small paw, just how much spring to give, and how deep to stick his claws in the bark. He did everything beautifully. But the leaves shook raindrops down his neck and made him bristle his whiskers.

He climbed a low branch and looked in at the kitchen window. There was Mrs. Tillie Todd rolling dough for the biscuits the Captain liked. She was little and round and cheerful-looking and wore a big flowered apron. When she saw the Cat, she began to laugh.

"You just better stay out there and get wet," she called. "It won't hurt you."

The Cat saw it was no use. Mrs. Tillie did not like him, and he knew very well she had several good reasons for it. He mewed one last mew, just in case she should change her mind. Then he gave her a look, and went down the lilac, headfirst. He knew now he'd have to wait until the Captain came back, but he wouldn't forget Mrs. Tillie's meanness—not he! He picked his way through the grass, lifting his feet high and walking around the puddles, and went in under the veranda by the little opening that only he knew about. There he sat, out of anyone's sight, switching his big black tail.

3

2

A Good Cat at Heart

About five o'clock the Captain came home. He was not a big man, but he carried a very big umbrella. He had wrinkles around his eyes from looking long distances, and he walked as though the street were going up and down under him, because he had spent so much of his time on the decks of boats. Everybody loved the Captain the moment they saw him because he was so kind and so jolly.

The Cat loved him, too, but took a naughty pride in not showing it, except sometimes when they were alone together. Then he would jump on the Captain's knee and rub his head against the Captain's chin, and go to sleep curled in

4

the hollow of his arm. And how careful the Captain would be not to move! They understood each other very well, and the Captain used to say that he had never shipped with a better shipmate than his black cat. But today the Cat was in a bad humor as he walked out from under the veranda.

"Well, well, there you are, hey?" said the Captain, and he opened the door and waited for the Cat to go in. But the Cat only looked at him. He was being provoking.

"Don't you want to go in?" asked the Captain.

The Cat still looked at him.

"All right," said the Captain, "if you won't, you won't, my lad," and he went in and started to shut the door.

But before he could get it shut the Cat came in.

5

It was a curious room, though neither the Cat nor the Captain thought so. It was both living room and dining room. There was a big fireplace of red brick with a Dutch oven at one side, and there were hooked rugs on the floor, some of them with designs of harbors or lighthouses on them. On the walls hung compasses and sea charts; and round glass balls (once used to float fishing nets) shone in the windows like big blue and white bubbles. A model of the Captain's first ship, the *Nautilus,* spread its sails high on the mantelpiece beyond reach of the Cat. There was a little boat in a bottle—it was a mystery how the masts and rigging ever got through the neck—and there were two pink conch shells from the West Indies.

In the window hung Jericho, the parrot. Poor Jericho had died a long time ago, before the Cat was so much as born. The Captain had been

6

fond of Jericho, and couldn't bear to think of looking up and not seeing him in his place. So Jericho was stuffed and there he still hung in his cage. Once a week Mrs. Tillie Todd opened the door of the cage and took Jericho out and carefully dusted him.

And Tillie kept all the brass in the room shining—the Captain was very particular about that. But neither the Captain nor Mrs. Tillie noticed that sometimes a few crumbs were left under the table. Only the Cat knew it.

When the Captain sat down and lighted his pipe, the Cat sat down, too, but instead of jumping into his chair opposite the Captain, he sat on the floor and watched the crumbs. It was very still except for the tick-tock-ticking of the cuckoo clock, and the steps of Tillie Todd getting supper ready in the kitchen. The Cat never stirred. After a long while, something moved

7

along the edge of the floor; something ran out on the carpet; something began to nibble a crumb.

Before you could have said, "Jack Robinson!" the Cat had that mouse by the neck.

The door into the kitchen was open a little, so in walked the Cat and dropped the mouse at Tillie Todd's feet. Some cats think that a mouse makes a nice present for the person they love, but this cat *knew* how Tillie felt about mice.

"Help! Fire! Murder! Police!" yelled Mrs. Tillie, climbing onto a kitchen chair as fast as she could scramble.

"Why, what's the trouble?" asked the Captain, stumping into the kitchen in a great hurry.

"He's climbing up the chair!" yelled Mrs. Tillie. "He's climbing up the chair!"

The mouse was far wiser than that. He had run back to his hole like lightning. But the Captain had to look under the chair, and up the chair legs, and then take a candle and hunt in all the corners of the kitchen before Mrs. Tillie would come down. Even then she was very much upset. Said she to the Captain, "If I had a cat like that, I wouldn't have him long!"

"He's really a good cat at heart," said the Captain sadly, for he always wanted the Cat and Mrs. Tillie to be friends. He couldn't understand why they didn't get on better and he scolded the Cat a little when they sat in their chairs by the fire. But the Cat treated the whole thing as an accident, and stretched his paws and looked at the Captain with big sleepy eyes and purred to himself as he listened to Tillie Todd singing crossly in the kitchen.

3

The Face at the Window

After supper, the Captain got out his spectacles, lighted his pipe, and began reading the newspaper. "Humph!" he would say sometimes; or, "Well, well!" or, perhaps, "They need some honest sailors in the Senate." But this evening he found something to read to the Cat. He always acted as though the Cat understood him, for it kept him from being lonely.

"Here's a poem," he said, looking up, "called 'The Bad Kittens.'" Then he read aloud slowly:

"You may call, you may call,
But the little black cats won't hear you,
The little black cats are maddened
By the bright green light of the moon.

They are running and whirling and hiding,
They are wild who were once so confiding,
They are mad when the moon is riding—
You will not catch the kittens soon!

"They care not for saucers of milk,
They care not for pillows of silk,
Your softest, crooningest call
Means less than the buzzing of flies.
They are seeing more than you see,
They are hearing more than you hear,
And out of the darkness they peer
With a goblin light in their eyes!"

But the Cat was not interested. He yawned. His mouth opened very wide, showing his sharp, curly tongue, and his whiskers stood out till they nearly touched in front of his nose. The Captain quite understood, and after that read to himself.

Tick-tock-tick went the cuckoo clock. The Cat's big eyes watched it. He knew that foolish

bobbing bird would soon pop out of his little door and call, "Cuckoo! cuckoo! cuckoo!" at the top of his lungs, and pop inside his little door again, slamming it behind him. He hated that cuckoo, but it had always been beyond his reach. Tonight he noticed that the big wing chair was nearer the clock than usual. Perhaps he could reach it if he ran across the rug, up the seat of the chair to the back, and so straight at the cuckoo. Well, it was worth trying. He waited. He was very patient. The Captain went on reading. At eight o'clock promptly the little door of the clock opened and out popped the wooden cuckoo.

"Cuckoo!" he began, bowing. "Cuckoo! Cu—" He didn't finish. There was a black rush across the rug, up the seat of the chair to the back, and so straight at the cuckoo. Then an awful crash! Down came the clock, the Cat, and the cuckoo, onto the floor all together.

14

"Bless my soul!" cried the Captain, jumping up. "Bless my soul!"

"Cuckoo! Cuckoo!" squawked the cuckoo.

The Cat said nothing, but hurried under the sofa when he saw the Captain coming. The Captain was a patient man, but he loved that clock.

"I'll teach you, you pirate!" he shouted, trying to reach him under the sofa. But whichever side of the sofa the Captain tried, the Cat always managed to be on the other. Finally the Captain, very red in the face, got down on his stomach to reach better. Tillie Todd heard him breathing hard, and stuck her head through the door.

"What's the trouble?" she asked, hoping that there was trouble.

But the Captain even now didn't want to admit how bad the Cat had been, especially to Mrs. Tillie.

"I'm looking for my handkerchief," he said, getting up, still very red in the face.

15

Tillie Todd began to giggle. "I bet that handkerchief is a good dodger!"

The Captain didn't say anything but sighed again and put the clock gently on the table, and went back to his chair. He looked at the clock sadly, and thought he would mend it in the morning when the light was better. When the Cat was sure that the Captain was quite settled again with his pipe and his paper, he came out from under the sofa, stretching and yawning as though he'd been having a nap. Somehow he wasn't very proud of himself, with the Captain feeling sad about the clock. But the Cat wasn't ready to admit how he felt yet.

Down on the hearth rug he sat to wash his paws.

Suddenly he had a feeling that he was being looked at. It couldn't be Mrs. Tillie. He had heard her go upstairs to bed. And it couldn't be the Captain, for he was puffing his pipe behind the newspaper. Quickly the Cat turned his head and looked at the window nearest the door. There was a face flattened against the pane, with eyes staring into the room. But before the Cat could see who or what it was, the face had disappeared, and nothing could be seen but the dark leaves of the white lilac bush still moving a little.

4

One Day on the "Lively Ann"

The first thing that the Cat did the next morning was to walk all around the outside of the house. The grass seemed more crushed than usual, as though someone else, heavier than the Cat, had also been there. The air was filled with the smell of honeysuckle and crimson rambler roses and wet grass and soft earth, and beyond all that the salt fragrance of the sea. All these the Cat was used to. The moment they opened the door both the Cat and the Captain could tell by the smell whether the breeze came over the harbor or across the hills. They didn't need even a glance at the schooner weather vane which spread its sails, no bigger than a handkerchief, above the roof of the toolshed. But this morning the Cat seemed to smell something strange. Perhaps it was a different tobacco. Perhaps it was boots. He couldn't be sure, but suddenly the odor brought back the memory of the most awful day in his life.

The year before, he had been with the Captain on the *Lively Ann* hauling lumber in the Caribbean. The weather was terribly rough for five days. The *Ann* was leaking, the waves were enormous, the wind howled all the time. The Mate of the ship was not an agreeable man at best, and he was less agreeable after five days of storm. He hadn't had any real sleep and he'd been too busy to eat much. He hadn't shaved, or even washed himself. His eyes were red with sleeplessness, his lips were blue with cold, and he was in a terrible temper when he happened to come on the ship's cat sitting comfortably washing his paws

in the cabin as though there were no storm at all. The sight infuriated him.

"You're the cause of all this tempest!" he cried. "Everyone knows that black cats bring bad luck on the sea. Overboard you go and we'll see if the wind won't shift!" With that he grabbed the Cat by the scruff of the neck and started for the deck.

"Mew!" cried the Cat. "Mew! mew! mew!"

Outside the waves were like the jaws of monsters waiting to swallow him up. They opened and shut their green mouths. They shot out their long, hungry, white tongues.

"Mew! mew! mew!" cried the Cat again. He was usually a brave cat, but now he was limp with helplessness and terror. But who was to hear him in all the noise and hurry? Who was to think of a cat in the midst of such a storm? Right to the rail went the Mate, and the Cat saw the waves reaching for him. But suddenly there were hurrying steps. Someone's fist shot out and hit the Mate on the chin. Down he fell, letting go the Cat as he went, and in a moment more the Cat was trembling but safe in the Captain's arms.

The Mate never forgave either of them for that blow, and when he left the ship at the next port he was scowling and muttering.

5

Every Fine Morning

Every fine morning at about ten, the Captain
went to the docks to see his vessel, the *Lively
Ann.* On the last voyage he had suffered a good
deal from rheumatism, and his married daughter had persuaded him to stay ashore for a year
or two. It was no distance from the house to the
wharves, and the Cat often watched the spar-
rows fly from the hedge to the rigging of the
schooners. When the Captain went to see the
Ann, the Cat went, too, walking ahead with his
tail proudly in the air. If he saw a dog, he stood
on his toes, ruffled up his hair, made his back
into an arch, and spat like a firecracker. The re-
sult was always the same. The dog would sud-

denly remember something he had left on the other side of the street, well out of reach. At that the Cat would give one last look and spit once more, daring him to come on, and then trot off again ahead of the Captain with his tail in the air.

When they got to the wharves, they both went aboard the *Lively Ann*. While the Captain walked about the deck seeing that everything was in place, the Cat tried to help by going down into the cabin and the hold to make sure that there were no rats. He was a silent cat. His little feet moved without a sound and his eyes were like two lanterns. He looked into every corner and smelled at every hole. It would take a brave rat to bring his family on board the *Lively Ann!*

When the Cat had made quite sure about rats, he went on deck again and sat by the door of the

ship's galley. Many a good dinner had he eaten there in past years. The last cook had liked to be by himself and do things at his own time in his own way. But he also knew how to be fond of his friends. He sometimes gave the Cat the nicest things to eat. The Cat liked him. Mrs. Tillie Todd gave him only what was left after she and the Captain had eaten the best of everything. He often had to sit and watch her putting into her mouth things he was sure he'd like for himself. He didn't think much of Mrs. Tillie, anyway.

While the Cat sat thinking about cooks, the Captain took a piece of newspaper out of his pocket (he always carried a great many things with him in case he might want them), unlocked his locker in the cabin, and took out a can of white paint and put it on the paper. It seemed to him that the rail looked a little shabby and he

26

loved to see the *Lively Ann* shipshape. He began painting the rail with a big brush. He was very careful not to get any paint on the deck. The Cat was curious. Pretty soon he *had* to jump on the rail to see what was going on.

"Scoot!" cried the Captain, and the Cat scooted. But every time he hit the deck, there were four little white paw marks of fresh paint. The Captain was cross, but the Cat was crosser. The paint stuck between his toes. He had to sit down and spread each paw like a fan and lick and bite all the paint off. And what faces he made at the taste of it!

When he was all clean again he lay on a pile of rope and watched the sea gulls. They had long wings, and big sliding shadows. They floated over his head and mewed almost like kittens. When a shadow passed very near him, he always got ready to spring at it. But he knew in his heart that no sea gull would ever come within reach. And he knew that he couldn't hold a shadow for all his claws. So after a while he grew tired of the sea gulls, and climbed out on the wharf to look through the cracks at the fish swimming about in the water below. When he saw one move, his eyes grew greedy and he licked his lips. He didn't even hear Mrs. Tillie ringing the dinner bell from the house.

But the Captain did. He straightened his back with the aid of his hands, for bending over made him feel his rheumatism. Then he put away the paint and the brush and looked for the Cat.

"I wonder," he said when he saw him watching the fish so hard, "why cats love fish and hate water?"

The Captain often asked himself questions he couldn't answer.

6

"There's Trouble Coming"

"There's trouble coming," said Mrs. Tillie as she was clearing away the dinner dishes.

"What makes you think so, Tillie?" asked the Captain politely.

"I had a black dream last night," said Mrs. Tillie, putting down her tray, "and this very morning I lost the four-leaf clover I carry. There's a chill down my spine and my knuckles crack. You take my word for it, Captain, trouble's coming this way."

"Maybe it's a storm," said the Captain and went to the window to look at the sky. The sky was very blue.

The Cat, too, was looking for trouble and he

29

was a cat who usually found it. What did he see, walking right across his own lawn, but a big long-haired yellow cat with a bell on his neck that went *ting-ting-ting* with every step he took. He was a very large cat, a very soft-looking cat, and a very foolish-looking cat, thought the Captain's Cat, getting between him and the gate.

"Grr," said the Captain's Cat, taking one step toward him on his tiptoes.

"Grr," said the other cat.

"Grrrr," said the Captain's Cat, taking another step.

"Grrrr," said the other cat.

"Grrrrr," said the Captain's Cat, taking still another step and looking him in the eye.

"Grrrrrr," said the yellow cat.

"Mrow," said the Captain's Cat, standing still and swelling larger and larger and waving his right front paw.

"Mrow," said the strange cat, swelling to twice his size and waving his left front paw.

"Mrow—meerow—meerowrow," said the Captain's Cat with his ears flat to his neck and a nasty look in his eye.

"Mrow—meerow—meerowrow," said the other cat just as loudly.

Then they both made a sound together, louder than any of all the loud sounds they had made before. There were spits in it, and growls, and snarls, and howls, and fireworks, and pinwheels, and screams, and screeches. Yet it was all one sound. There was even a ringing of the bell on the yellow cat's collar. The noise was very loud. At the same instant the two cats jumped at each other and rolled over and over. They looked like one animal, all legs, and tails, and teeth. They bit and they scratched and they kicked. The Captain's Cat got his mouth full of yellow fur. He had to spit it out before he could get another bite. He tore the pretty little bell off the yellow cat's ribbon. He got his teeth in his ear. And all the time he was making terrible scary noises, even with his mouth full of fur. The yellow cat wasn't doing so well. He was so beautiful that he spent most of the day on a soft cushion and had cream for breakfast from a yellow bowl. He wasn't used to fighting.

"Meow," he cried, and suddenly leaped free from the Captain's Cat, and ran away with his ear bleeding and his little bell gone from the ribbon around his neck.

The Captain's Cat watched him go and licked a scratch on his nose. Then he looked at the house to see if anyone had seen the fight. He was not a good cat. He was proud of his rough ways. Sure enough, there was Mrs. Tillie's head bobbing in one window, and the Captain's gray head in another. The Cat was glad they had seen him.

"You ought to be ashamed of yourself," said Mrs. Tillie, opening the door.

In walked the Cat pleasantly. He had been looking for trouble and he had found it. He was satisfied. He was satisfied even with Tillie Todd. Perhaps this was the trouble she thought was coming. Perhaps not. He didn't care. He could take care of any trouble that dared come along! He went to his saucer. There was no milk in it. Then he was not so well satisfied. But Tillie was busy and paid no attention to him. She was baking little cakes for tea. They smelled delicious. She put them on the table and began to stir the frosting in a yellow bowl.

The Cat mewed for milk, but Tillie went on stirring.

The Cat was glad when the doorbell rang. Out of the kitchen went Mrs. Todd, tying on a clean apron as she went. Up on a stool leaped the Cat, and up on his hind legs he stood, and scooped one paw into the bowl of frosting. He licked it. In went the paw again. But at that moment the front door slammed and made him jump. Down came the bowl, frosting and all, on top of him, and before he got over the scare of that, in came Tillie Todd, running. She gave one look and reached for the broom. Away went the Cat with Tillie and the broom after him. Across the living room, and up the stairs, into the Captain's room (upsetting a chair), across the little hall. To his surprise, the door was open into the spare chamber, so in the Cat tore with Tillie close behind. There was frosting in his eyes, but he could see an open window (usually the spare chamber was kept tight as a drum unless Tillie Todd was cleaning it) and through that open window he sailed, just in the nick of time. Down came the broom with a thud, but it only hit the very least and littlest tip of his tail.

7

Sh! What's That?

The Cat sat on the roof of the veranda, licking frosting off his coat. He always liked things to be neat, so he had a good deal of washing to do on his busy days. But the frosting was delicious —not at all like the paint. The sun was shining. Two or three birds sang, "Cheer up, cheer up," in a tree nearby. It was on just such days that the Cat enjoyed sitting all alone by himself on the roof, quietly watching everything.

Yet somehow this afternoon he was worried. He remembered the face at the window last night, and the smell in the morning which made him think of the Mate, and the door and window of the spare chamber which he had found so unexpectedly open. He felt responsible, for he alone had noticed these things, and he could tell no one of his anxiety, not even the Captain. If only Tillie Todd had not shut the window behind him, he would have visited all the rooms to see if anything was wrong with them. He was worried. He kept washing his whiskers long after the last bit of frosting was off them. He got a whisker down his throat and nearly coughed his head off. He got a whisker up his nose and nearly sneezed his head off. Then he stopped washing his whiskers and went to look in the windows of the spare chamber. Everything seemed in place. There was nothing more that he could do for the time being but forget about it.

From where he lay, he could see out over the harbor and watch the sails moving, and hear the put-put-put of the motor launches. Once a sea gull flew over him with a fish hanging out of its bill. Several times he heard steps on the street and people went by. He watched everything they did, but they never saw him lying on the roof, with his toes sedately tucked in under his white shirt front.

About four o'clock the Captain's married daughter and her little boy turned in at the gate. They were coming for tea. They, too, passed right under the Cat but never thought to look up. He was looking down at them, though. He saw the flowers on the hat of the Captain's daughter, and the paper pinwheel Ted was carrying. He heard them knocking at the door and Tillie Todd opening it suddenly, just the way the cuckoo used to open his little door.

The Cat stayed where he was. He hadn't been invited.

But suddenly he heard another sound. It was like a step in the spare chamber. Sh! What's that? The Cat ran to the window, but he could see nothing unusual. Everything seemed in its place. Perhaps the Captain had come upstairs to get a handkerchief.

8

The Cat's First Party

Tillie Todd brought in the tea on a big red tray from China. The teapot was shaped like an elephant with steam coming from his trunk. Ted loved it. The milk came in a pitcher like a bright brown cow with her tail curled for a handle. Ted was so little he sat on a stool near the fire and held his cup in both hands. The grown-up people drank real tea, but Ted had only a spoonful of tea mixed with a great deal of milk.

Mrs. Tillie smiled. She loved tea parties. She had made little cookies shaped like fish with caraway seeds for eyes, and big cookies filled with raisins, and cupcakes. But the cupcakes didn't have any frosting on them because most of the frosting was on the kitchen floor, and the rest was inside the Cat. Tillie told the Captain's daughter just how bad that cat was.

"We must call him for Ted to play with," said the Captain's daughter, who always laughed at Tillie Todd's stories of the Cat.

"You'd best leave him where he is, ma'am," said Tillie.

"Oh, cats are always good with little children," said the Captain's daughter, who knew a great deal about cats.

"Kitty, kitty," said Ted, who had been listening.

"Well, well, where is he?" asked the Captain, pleased that they wanted to see his cat.

"He was walking right on air the last I saw of him," said Tillie with a sniff.

The Captain opened the door and called: "Here, kitty, kitty, kitty! Here, kitty, kitty, kitty! Come, puss, puss, puss!"

The Cat's head appeared over the edge of the veranda roof. He was delighted at being called, but he tried to appear unconcerned. He looked at the Captain, then slid down the veranda pillar, walked into the house, passed Tillie as though he didn't see her, and went right up to the Captain's daughter. She knew what cats like. She tickled him under the chin and rubbed his back and sang nonsense to him under her breath:

"Cat, Cat, it's perfectly evident
  You are a black cotton cat,
 And your eyes are a pair of underclothes' buttons
  Sewed on with a black thread, at that.

"Cat, Cat, it's perfectly evident
  Your whiskers are made out of string.
 Someone's tangled up those on the left of your nose
  Which I think is a rather good thing.

"And, Cat, that magnificent pout of your chest
  Just shows how the sawdust's stuffed in it!
 I think you could act as a little doorstop—
  At least for the half of a minute!"

At first when Ted came near, the Cat ran away. He had never seen him before, and he thought Ted must be a man who was very little. He wasn't used to children anyway, and seeing such a *very* little man reaching out such a *very* little hand somehow scared him.

But pretty soon he got used to it. Ted poured milk from the brown cow's mouth into a saucer. Then the Cat settled down neatly and very carefully lapped up the milk, keeping his whiskers dry. The last drop was on his chin. He licked it off, wet the back of his right paw to smooth his shining fur, and then lightly jumped up on the Captain's lap and poked his head under the Captain's hand to be petted, which was very unusual for him to do in company. Ted leaned against the Captain's knee to listen to the Cat purring. It was better than the ticking of a watch.

"How happy they all look," thought the Cap-

tain's daughter. "It would make a pretty picture."

"His engine's going," said Ted, thinking of his father's car, and they all laughed.

But the grownups began talking about other things and the Cat grew sleepy and forgot to purr. "His engine's stopped," said Ted in his little voice. But the Captain didn't hear exactly what he said and only patted him on the back and said, "Yes, yes," kindly.

The Cat's big black tail, with a little curl at the tip of it, hung near Ted's hand.

"I'll pull this lever," said Ted helpfully. If only the Captain had heard that time! But again he just said, "Yes, yes," and went on talking with his daughter.

Ted gave one good pull and then everything happened at once.

The Cat yowled.

The Captain said, "Bless my soul!" in a loud voice.

The Captain's daughter cried, "What did you do, Ted?"

Ted began dropping tears on five pink scratches on his hand.

Mrs. Tillie popped her head in at the door, and then, without any questions, ran for the broom. It was really unfair of Tillie, for the Cat had meant to be as good as gold at his very first tea party.

9

This Cat Saved Us

Before going to bed at night the Captain always wrote in his log book. A log book is the diary of a ship at sea and the Captain pretended to himself that his house was a ship. He was more used to ships than to houses.

"This day comes in fair with light westerly breeze," he wrote carefully.

"At four bells, morning watch (which is the sea way of saying ten o'clock in the morning), boarded the *Lively Ann*. Found all shipshape. Painted rail.

"During the afternoon watch, some trouble in the galley (that referred to Tillie's chasing the Cat with a broom).

"At eight bells received on board the mate and cabin boy of the brig *Garfield* (that was his daughter's married name). Tea for all hands.

"At eight bells, evening watch, wind freshened, backed to NE. Saw all serene for the night.

"So ends this day."

The Captain wished he could say how far the house had sailed, but he knew it had stayed in its own yard behind its white paling fence. The log book of a house is not half so exciting as a ship's. He sighed as he closed the book. Then he locked the door, looked at all the windows, wound the grandfather's clock, and put the screen around the fire. The Cat still lay in his chair and made no move to go upstairs. He often waited until the embers were cool before he curled up on his rug in the Captain's room.

It didn't take the Captain long to get into bed. For that matter he didn't have a bed, because a bed never stirs during the night. He slept in a hammock that swung a little when he turned over and reminded him of the sea. He was so sleepy that he paid no attention when he saw the Cat come to his door, hesitate, and then turn toward the spare chamber instead of coming in as usual. He turned out the light, tumbled into his hammock, and was almost asleep when he heard a mewing. Still he paid no attention.

"Mew, mew!" went the Cat.

"Do let me go to sleep," muttered the Captain from his pillow.

"Mew, mew!" went the Cat.

The Captain pulled the blankets over his ears. He couldn't bear to be disturbed just now.

"Mew, mew, mew!" went the Cat and jumped on the hammock.

"Mew, mew!" went the Cat, scratching at the blankets.

"Well, well!" said the Captain, wide awake at last. "Whatever is the matter with you this evening?"

At that, down jumped the Cat, ran to the door, ran back to the Captain again, and then to the door. His hair was ruffled. His whiskers were bristling. His eyes were green. The Captain, who had turned on the light, saw that something was wrong. He put on his dressing gown and picked up his cane. Across the little hall went the Cat and into the spare chamber and up to the door of the clothes closet.

"Mrow," went the Cat, looking very frightened, but brave.

The Captain opened the door carefully.

And there hidden in the closet was the Mate.

The Captain had quite a hard time before he finally got the Mate tied up with the clothesline Mrs. Tillie brought. The Cat jumped up on the bureau to keep out of harm's way. Tillie Todd, in a pink flannel nightdress, stood in the doorway until the Captain sent her to telephone for the police.

"He evidently had a grudge against you, Captain," said the policeman later, "and was waiting for you to go to sleep. He must have gotten in through an upper window during the day. When the house was quiet and you were asleep he'd have come out and robbed you and maybe worse, too."

"I *was* almost asleep," said the Captain. "It was this cat here who saved us. He came into my room and made me wake up, and led me to this door. He must have heard or seen something after I went to bed."

Then everyone turned and looked at the Cat who was still sitting on the bureau and who couldn't help feeling proud. Even Tillie Todd

knew at last that the Captain was right. This *was* a good cat, a very good cat. After what had happened, she could never be angry with him again. When Tillie begged anyone's pardon she did it thoroughly.

"I want to apologize to you right here and now for the mean things I've said about you," she said, shaking the Cat by the paw.

"I always knew he was a good cat," said the Captain happily. The Cat jumped down and rubbed against Tillie Todd's ankles to show that he, too, could forget any little misunderstandings. Then he looked at his friend, the Captain, as though asking for something, and ran to the top of the stairs.

The policeman was just going to leave with his prisoner, but he couldn't take his eyes off the Cat. "He wants something to eat," said the policeman.

"He can have anything he wants in this house," said the Captain, starting for the stairs.

Mrs. Tillie didn't say anything, but before the Captain was halfway down she hurried to the refrigerator. And the beautiful long slice of white chicken meat she had put away as a special treat for herself went into the Cat's saucer.

But delicious as the chicken was, the Cat did not drop his chin to eat at once. First he took a long, slow look about the room. There was the Captain looking at him with his usual affection and even more than his usual pride. There was Mrs. Tillie Todd looking at him with gratitude and apology. The officer had stopped near the outer door to give the Cat a final glance of admiration, and standing beside him was the Mate, now in handcuffs, looking at him with pure hatred and cursing under his breath. The Cat stared back at the Mate with real enjoyment.

Then, having satisfied himself that he was indeed the center of everyone's attention, the Cat at last gave a "prrrp" of satisfaction and, dropping his head, began to eat.